A few more
frogs for my
daughter
Sandy Calder

Sylvester

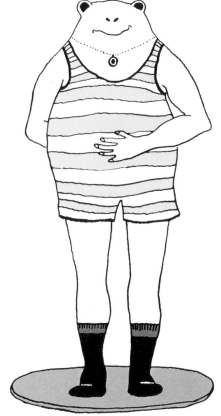

WRITTEN AND ILLUSTRATED BY

Sandra Calder Davidson

Translated from the French by Alexander Calder, Jean Davidson, and Judy Hyun

FOLLETT PUBLISHING COMPANY **Chicago   New York**

A special art edition of this book has been published by Maeght, Paris.

Library of Congress Catalog Card Number: 67-15023   First Printing   T/L 8410

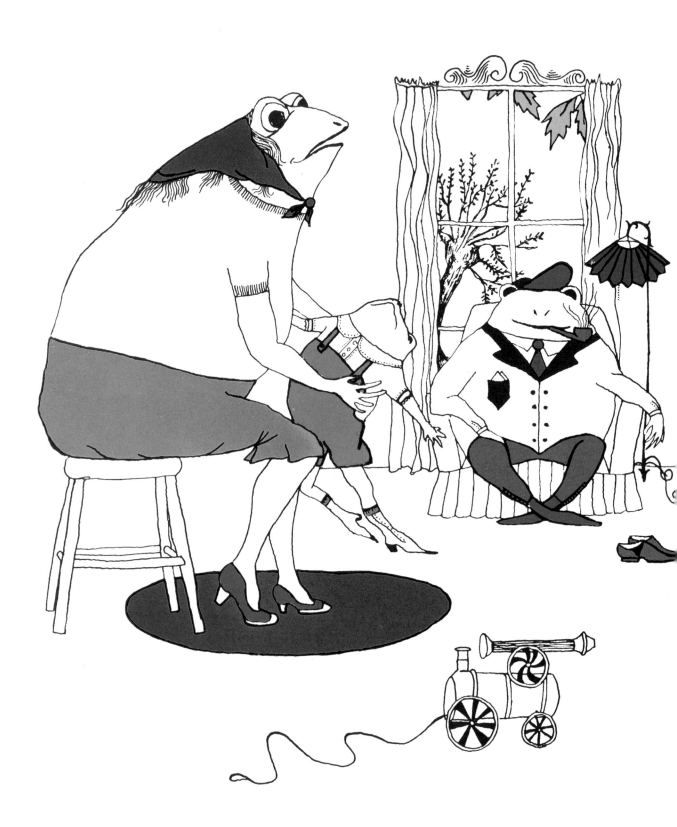

Sylvester is three years old today.

"Now," says his father, "you must learn to swim. All frogs swim at your age."

Sylvester stamps his foot, and cries, "I don't like water. I won't swim."

His mother is upset. "You are a frog. You must learn to swim."

His father smiles, and says: "We'll have a picnic, a swimming party, on the banks of Raindrop Pond."

So, on this beautiful autumn day, Sylvester, his father and mother, his uncles and aunts, and his cousins are on their way to the pond, carrying baskets filled with fruits and cakes, bread and cheese.

A large box tied with bright red ribbon catches Sylvester's eye. "I wish, I wish it were for me!" he thinks.

But his parents' words fill him with the chill of cold water: "You must learn to swim."

"The sky," Sylvester says to himself, "is for the birds to fly through, the fields are to run in; water is to drink, but not for frogs to swim in; picnics are for frogs and presents are for me."

It is a happy day for Sylvester. Despite the prospect of a dip, he is very excited.

At the pond's edge, his mother hands him the large box, and everyone says, "Happy Birthday, Sylvester!"

Wide-eyed, Sylvester opens the package with trembling hands. "What a beautiful present! A bathing suit! Perfect for swimming!"

But where are they?

They are flying into the water.

"Like birds!" says Sylvester. "They fly like birds. They swim like fish. But I am neither fish nor bird. I am a frog!"

The colorful stripes of their bathing suits crisscross the water.

They urge him to jump in.

Oh, no, no, no! Poor Sylvester dares not jump.

"A red fish named Basil wants to play with you," shouts his father.

"Play with me? I love to play." And without thinking, he rushes to the pond and plunges in.

Basil roars with laughter.

"He jumped," cries his father, happily.

"With his boots on!" sighs his mother.

They all wait impatiently, but Sylvester does not float to the surface.

While little bubbles burst on the surface, Sylvester sinks and sinks and sinks. "I'll soon touch bottom," he sighs helplessly. "I don't even drink water, and now I am soaked to the skin." Out of the corner of his tearful eye he glimpses little fish making fun of him.

"Ugh, those slimy beasts with spikes and claws . . . I hate them all. That naughty red fish! That Basil! I'll never play with him again!"

Overhead, his mother says anxiously, "It's a good start, but we must pull him out!"

"I'll go!" says Basil, and dives into the depths.

Cold feet and a high fever keep Sylvester in bed the next day; comfortably installed amid pillows and quilts, he sits sipping hot lemonade.

Neighbors drop in to ask about him.

"How is he?"

"Did he learn to swim?"

"Heavens no!" says Sylvester's mother.

And, overnight, he becomes known as Sylvester the Leaden Frog.

As days pass, Sylvester becomes more and more interested in Basil. "As soon as I am well, I'll go talk to him. But I won't play with him."

As he gazes fondly on his new bathing suit, Sylvester wonders what Basil is doing and where he lives.

Then one day Basil comes to call.

"Here are some flowers . . . for your speedy recovery," says Basil. "If you want swimming lessons, you'll always find me at the pond. Good-by for now."

That night, Sylvester turns and twists and tosses in bed.

"Red"—he dreams of the color red.

At the crack of dawn he slips out of bed and dresses in red.

"Red is the color that makes one float! It is the color of Basil's coat!" Sylvester sings as he speeds toward Raindrop Pond.

By the time Sylvester finds Basil the sun is already up. They are very happy to see each other, and sit down side by side on the dock. Up since dawn, Sylvester is hungry. He pulls out bread, jam and bananas from his bag.

"Sylvester," orders Basil, "put away that food! First swimming lesson: never eat before swimming. Now, put on your bathing suit. You are built like a frog. You are a frog. So S W I M like a frog!"

"I am a frog," thinks Sylvester, and quite confidently dives in.

"Down he goes! Down he goes!" sing the little fish in chorus.

Sylvester panics. "What shall I do?" he weeps, "my poor wet shoes! My bag . . ."

Above, Basil watches closely. "Sylvester really is too fat." Then Basil dives down to snatch a weeping Sylvester from the pond's weeds.

"Don't be too discouraged, Sylvester. We will try again tomorrow."

The next morning it is still dark when Sylvester arrives at the pond.

"Today, let's try another way: a little less swimming and a lot more play. Climb on my back and we'll go around and around!" commands Basil.

"This is real swimming," sings Sylvester, as the wind whistles in his ears. "I love to swim!"

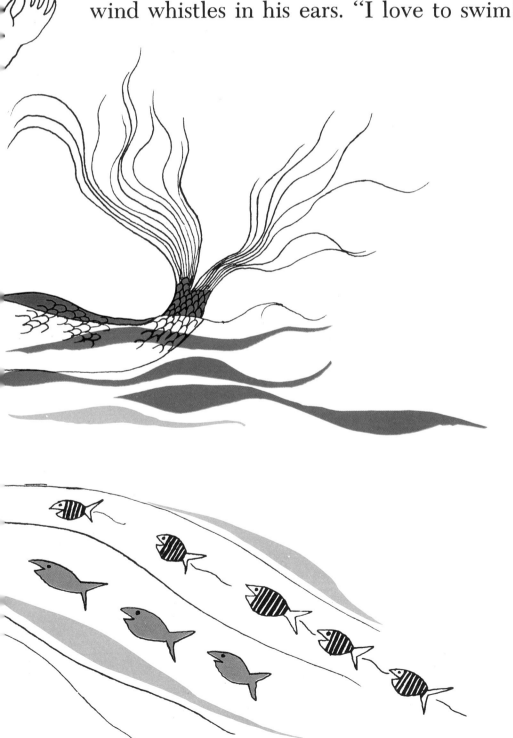

"I'm swimming! I'm swimming! If my parents could see me, they'd sing with me! I swim like a fish! I fly like a bird! And whistle like the wind! I am a shining knight in armor charging through the enemy lines!"

But Basil soon pants: "Out of breath! I am out of breath! That's all for now!"

"See you soon!" yells Sylvester, galloping back home.

The next morning Max the Postman finds Sylvester on his rocking-horse.

"I'm swimming! I'm swimming!" he exclaims.

"Really?" says Max. "Can such a fat frog swim? I have a very important letter addressed directly to Master Sylvester Serge."

Max and Sylvester sit down side by side to read the impressive letter.

The Champion Swimming Club...

Master Sylvester Serge:

The Champion Swimming Club announces a speed race at Raindrop Pond in exactly one week.

We invite you, Master Sylvester Serge, to participate.

The first race will begin at nine in the morning.

Counting on your participation, I am

Sincerely yours,

CHAIRMAN

SWIM FOREVER

Sylvester jumps for joy, "What a magnificent letter! What beautiful paper!" Already Sylvester imagines himself to be a champion.

"I'm going to be a champion, but champions have to train. There is not a minute to lose," Sylvester tells his mother as he dashes off to find Basil.

Sylvester finds Basil at the gym. Dozens of other athletes are training too; doing push-ups, chinning themselves, walking the tightrope, doing cart-wheels, weight-lifting, playing leap-frog and practicing many difficult feats.

All the swimmers in training are muscular and strong.

"This is worth seeing," thinks Sylvester. "I have too much fat and no muscle! I must lose weight. I must train first by myself!"

And Sylvester slips out unnoticed . . .

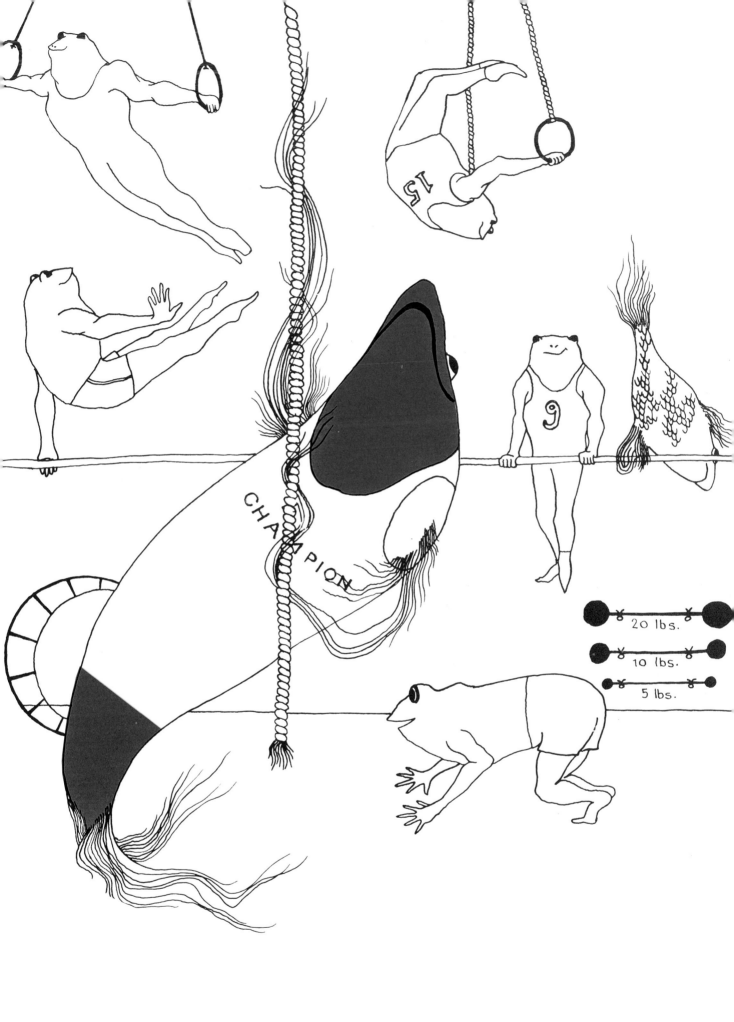

At home Sylvester stands before his mother's big mirror.

"All fat! No muscles! The opposite of all champions!"

And before the day is over . . .

Sylvester has brought down from the attic all his father's old sporting equipment: Boxing gloves, punching-bag, sandbag, weights, golf clubs, football, a bow and arrows, and even two javelins.

Sylvester wraps an old woolen scarf around his middle and begins his physical fitness week.

"All fat and no muscles," repeats Sylvester as he socks the punching-bag.

At meal time, Sylvester sits by himself to avoid the temptation of his mother's delicious cooking. And as soon as he finishes his meal of raw vegetables and fresh fruits, it is time for more exercise.

FIRST LIKE THIS

AND THEN LIKE THAT!

Soon Sylvester invents the Swimming Machine. This machine is made from a large elastic belt hooked to the ceiling. Thus, hanging in space, Sylvester gets the feel of swimming without having to get wet.

Between training sessions he observes his body's progress in his mother's mirror. Much to his satisfaction, muscles appear here and there.

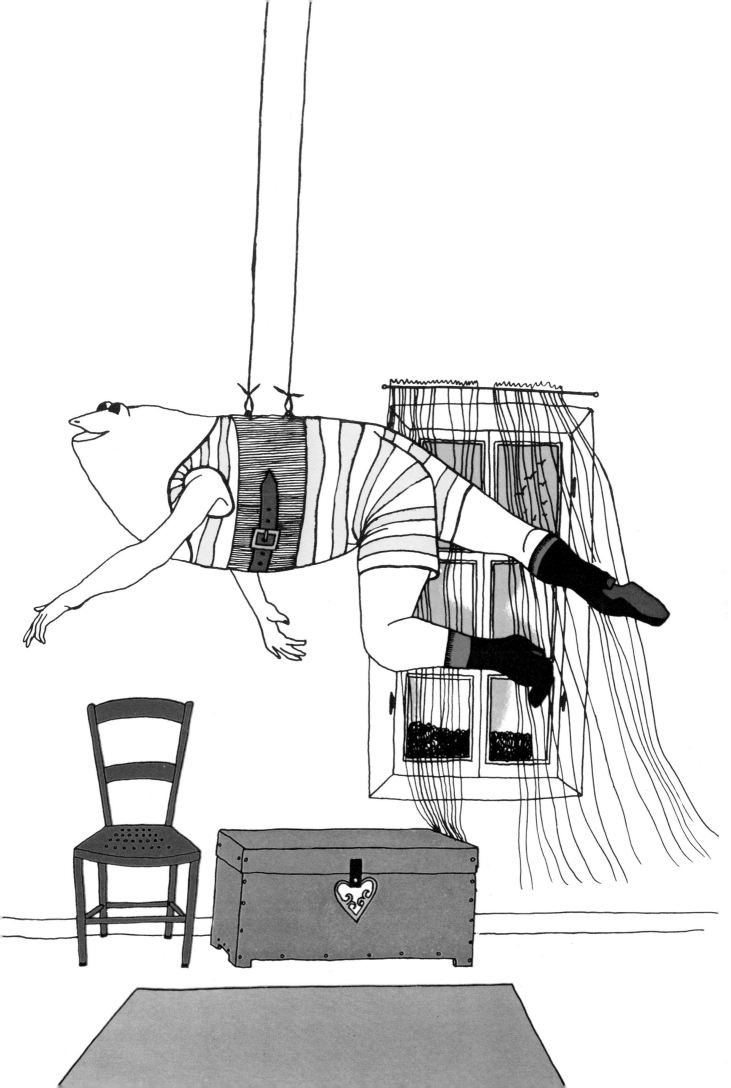

On the eve of the championship, Sylvester lies down on the edge of Raindrop Pond. The moon is red above his head. He watches the reeds sway and the light on the water and thinks of his beautiful bathing suit—the suit of a champion.

And gazing tenderly at the water, Sylvester falls into a deep sleep.

"What time can it be?" Sylvester jumps. People are gathering at the pond's edge. "Time for a snack," he thinks, and then remembers Basil's first lesson: "Never eat before swimming."

Sylvester can see Max the Postman, the baker,
Mrs. Wren, the gardener and even the press; hundreds
are gathering at the pond's edge. He rushes to find
the starting line . . .

The Chairman is already standing on his platform, his hat in one hand and a loudspeaker in the other. A burst of applause resounds across the pond. Eyes skyward, he waits for silence, then he speaks:

"Ladies and gentlemen, dear children: I am delighted to see you on this lovely autumn day. You all know why you are gathered here. We will soon find among our sporting friends the winner. It is now two minutes to nine. At exactly nine the bell will ring, then our champions will jump into the water!"

The bell rings! They are off! Sylvester plunges in immediately. He braces his feet against the bank and pushes with all his might. The little fish watch the Leaden Frog.

"Down he goes! Down he goes!" they sing in chorus.

Sylvester pays no attention. "I can only do my best," says Sylvester, putting into motion all the muscles of his champion's body.

And to everyone's surprise, including his own, Sylvester does not sink.

He kicks, he churns, he breathes in, he blows out, he gurgles, he splashes, he moves forward . . . Sylvester is warming up. He gathers speed. He even loses sight of the little fish. He loses track of everyone.

"The dragonflies from the other bank are coming to greet me. The water is shallow. I must be nearing the goal," he says to himself. He raises his head in a last effort and sees a banner floating overhead: FINISH.

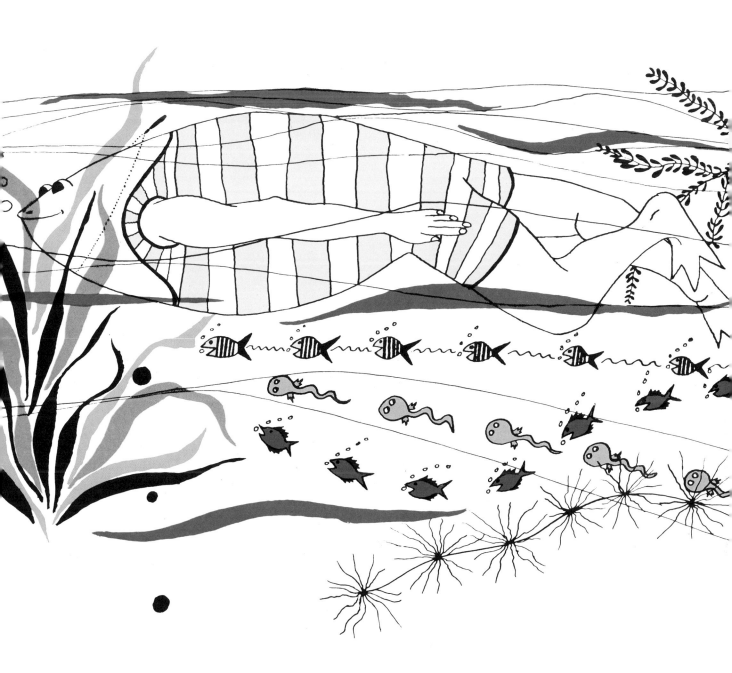

"He is the fastest swimmer," cry the tadpoles breathlessly.

"He is our champion," shout the minnows.

Still dripping, Sylvester climbs onto the platform. No one has ever seen a Leaden Frog swim so fast!

"Here is our champion," cries the Chairman through his loud speaker, as he places the wreath around Sylvester's neck. "He is our youngest champion ever."

Sylvester speaks to the cheering crowd: "I am the champion, I knew it all along. But all the same it is a big surprise. It is really thanks to my friend, Basil. I am very, very happy!"

After everyone has congratulated Sylvester he goes home with his family.

That evening, the family portrait over the fireplace is replaced by Sylvester's wreath.

"My! How you have grown!" exclaims his mother.

"Tell me a story," begs Sylvester.

She tells him the story of a frog who could not swim.

"What a ridiculous frog!" laughs Sylvester. "A frog that couldn't swim! Was I ever as ridiculous as that frog?"

"Of course not, Sylvester. You are not ridiculous. You are a champion!" They all laugh heartily while Sylvester gets into bed.

"Mother," whispers Sylvester, "tomorrow morning I'm going to get up early and teach that poor frog to swim."

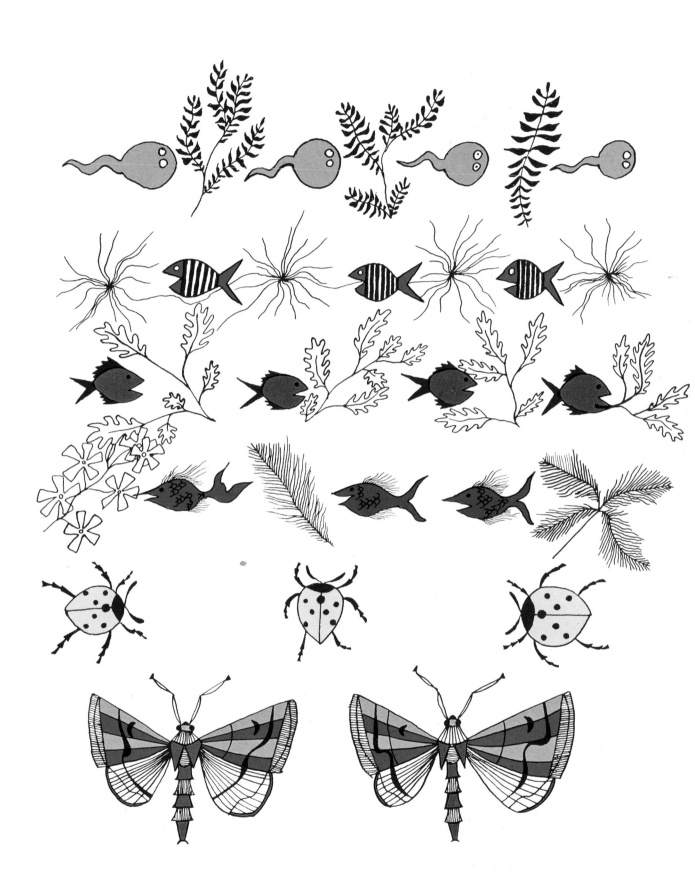